How John Became a Man:
Life Story of a Motherless Boy

Isabel C. Byrum

Contents

CHAPTER I

The Prairie Pasture

Out on the prairie in one of the western states where buffaloes and wild horses once had roamed at their pleasure and where cacti and yuccas still thrived and bloomed could be seen a small two-story frame building. There was nothing strange in this except that the house was different from the average house of the plains; for at this particular time the greater part of the dwellings were made of sod, mud, and brush.

The people, generally speaking, were of that type who think principally of getting all the enjoyment from their everyday lives that it is possible to obtain. There was, therefore, little thought among them of the hereafter, when men must give an account of themselves before a just and living God. In fact, the younger generation scarcely knew that there was a God who took note of all their ways.

The building, so different from the ordinary dwellings upon the prairie, was the home of a tiny lad named John. It was a happy home; for both his parents were living, and the love that bound their hearts together brought peace and happiness to each member of the little household. But could this happy group have known of the presence of a grim monster just outside the door, who at that very moment was seeking an entrance, their joy would have given place to sorrow. Death was soon to destroy the light and comfort of that home. The devoted wife and mother was not strong; and after a severe illness lasting but a few short days, her spirit left the ones she loved and her lifeless body was carried to its last resting place in the cemetery a few miles away.

Little John was, of course, too young to realize the true meaning of the change; but that something dreadful had happened he very well knew, and his large pathetic eyes spoke the grief that he did understand and could not express. During the three years of his short life he had known the care of a tender, loving mother, whose ambitions were high and noble. Although not a Christian, she had often expressed her wish that her little brown-eyed boy might grow up to be an honor to his father and mother, and a blessing to his country. After her death his papa's eyes were often filled with tears, for he loved and pitied his little boy.

One evening when the lights were dim and the hands of the clock were pointing to the bedtime hour, John felt his father's arms tenderly encircled about him and heard him softly saying: "My little John, we are left all alone now, and you must hurry up and become a man as soon as you can; for I need you to help me. Mama has gone away and left us, and she cannot teach you the things that she had planned that you should know; so we will have to do the best that we can, but you must help me. First of all, I want you to learn how to pray; for there is a God in heaven, who made you, and of whom your mother expected to tell you. Before Him we should bow down and pray every night before we go to sleep."

"Does He hear all the words we say?" asked little John in an awed tone, quite unable to comprehend his father's meaning, "and does He look at us when we are asleep?"

"Yes," his father answered; "God sees and knows everything. Now, I will tell you the short prayer that I used to say when I was a little boy like you—the prayer that my mother taught me."

Thus it was that John, kneeling beside his little bed repeated the prayer that has been lisped by thousands of other baby voices:

"Now I lay me down to sleep;
I pray thee, Lord, my soul to keep.
If I should die before I wake,
I pray thee, Lord, my soul to take."

As the days and weeks sped by, John thought often of his dear mama and wished that he might see her; but he as often would recall his father's words to be a little man, and with all his strength he endeavored to be what he considered a man ought to be. But although he tried, in his childish way, to be one, he was often very lonely; and had it not been for frequent visits to his uncle's home, several miles distant, he would have missed his precious mother even more than he did. While at his uncle's, he could play with his two cousins, Will and Charley. At last it was decided that it would be best for John and his father to go and make their home with the uncle until John was older.

Now Charley was just about John's age; but as Charley was a cripple, John had chosen Will, who was several years the oldest, to be his closest friend and companion. Regardless of these facts, however, the three boys generally played together. Their playground was the vast dooryard extending far out over the prairie.

In time they were given the responsibility of herding the cows. To herd the cows meant to see that the cattle did not wander about in the neighborhood corn, wheat, and barley fields that were scattered about here and there over the prairies and that were in but few instances fenced, and to see that they were driven to some water-place at certain intervals and were brought home at the milking hour.

The watering places were known as "buffalo-wallows," for they had been made by the buffalos in wallowing. These basins were usually kept filled with water by the rains. Some of the "wallows," or "ponds," were rather deep, and were treacherous because of sudden "drop-offs"; but they were usually shallow, and it was generally safe for the children to play along the edge.

After the first sharp edge of his grief was dulled, John's father did not feel it so keenly his duty to instruct his child and to teach him to reverence his Creator; and when John was about six years of age, the father was kept so busy with his work that he had but little time to spend with the child. John's aunt, too, although a good woman, was too much occupied with housekeeping to do her duty by her own two boys, much less by a third. So John and his cousins had spent nearly all of the three years that they had been together in doing as they pleased, and in finding as much enjoyment in living as it was possible for them to find. It was, therefore, not strange that they had learned and invented many new ways to get amusement, and that some of these were evil; for Satan, as he always does in such cases, had lent them a helping hand.

The work of attending to the cows did not, of course, occupy nearly all their time, and the boys found it great sport to play around the wallows and in them.

On one occasion Will said:

"Say, boys, did you ever hear the story about the man who walked upon the water? I don't remember just how the story went; but I heard somebody say that the man's name was Jesus, and that another man got out of a boat to go and meet Him. The first fellow did all right, but the second one came very near drowning because he looked down at the water. Maybe he wanted to see how deep the water was, and I guess he would have got drowned if they hadn't been close to the shore. Now, I am going to do like Jesus did. Want to see me?"

Naturally both the boys wanted to see him perform a feat like that, and Will quickly scampered into the water. Now, the wallow was very shallow all the way across, and Will was soon on the opposite side. The smaller boys, not knowing the depth of the water, supposed that it was deep and that Will had actually done some marvelous thing. Will did not know that he was doing wrong by speaking lightly of one of the Savior's miracles; for he had never been in Sunday-school, and his parents had not taught him the sacredness of the words and acts of the Savior. He simply wanted to play a joke on his companions.

The smaller boys talked the matter over when they were alone, and John said:

"Say, Charley, what do you suppose held Will up the other day on that water? That wallow must have been deep out in the middle. Let's try it some time for ourselves when Will isn't around. I believe we could do it as well as he did."

Charley was agreed, and the two smaller lads watched their chance. One day when Will was not with them, they chose a wallow that they thought would answer their purpose. "I'll go first," Charley said, and he hurried forward as rapidly as his little crippled limb could carry him, to the water's edge and out into the pond.

Suddenly poor little Charley disappeared. John saw his cousin as he went down into the deep water, and realized his danger. He knew that something must be done and done at once, and with a bound he sprang in after his companion. He did not, however, go beyond the shallow water, and when his cousin came to the surface, he reached out his hand and caught him by the hair; and as Charley had not lost the power to help himself, he was soon able, by John's assistance, to scramble to a place of safety.

The boys decided that they would say nothing about the accident; and as they remained away from the house long enough for Charley's clothing to dry, no questions were asked. But was the scene unnoticed? No. He who notes the sparrow's fall was watching over these little boys; He had not forgotten John's little prayer that had been taught him by his father. God was caring for these little untaught children in that vast prairie pasture.

CHAPTER II
In the Sod Cellar

Almost without exception the homes on the prairies were provided with sod cellars. Even the few modern dwellings in the community in which John's uncle lived were not without these old-fashioned cellars, which served as a protection in times of storms and tornadoes. The cellars served also as places in which to store the fruits and vegetables for winter use. And very often, too, a large quantity of tobacco leaves that had been dried and kept back when the summer's crop was sold could be discovered in one of these places.

The home of John's uncle was provided with just such a cellar—a deep hole dug in the ground and covered over with a dense roofing of brush, mud, and sod. Within this cellar a large supply of tobacco leaves had been stored. John had been in the cellar many times. He knew the tobacco was there, and he knew to what use his uncle put the tobacco. He knew also that his cousin Will both chewed and smoked the leaves, but it had not occurred to him that he himself could do so.

The reason why he had not thought of using it was perhaps that his father had once told him that the using of tobacco was a bad habit and urged him to let it alone. But the fact that he had not been tempted did not guarantee that he would not be; the fact that he had no appetite for tobacco did not conclusively prove that he would never acquire one; nor did the fact that he had been told to let tobacco alone warrant that he would need no further watching—for an unforeseen temptation was lurking near.

One day when John went into the cellar with his cousin Will, his cousin filled a pipe with the leaves and offered it to him, bidding him smoke. John shook his head, and said that he did not want to smoke, for his father had said that using tobacco was a bad habit and that it would ruin his health.

"Then, why does he use it himself?" Will reasoned. "Do you suppose that he would use it if he thought that it was going to hurt him? Now, John, look here; you said that you wanted to become a man. Here's your chance. If you get to where you can smoke a pipe, chew tobacco, and spit, in the way that your father and my dad do, you will be a man. Just some folks' saying that it is a bad habit doesn't need to make any difference with you."

As John thought over his cousin's words, they did seem reasonable, and he remembered that all the men he had ever seen used tobacco. So he decided that, if he expected to be a man himself, he must soon begin to use it, too. He therefore accepted the pipe and began to puff vigorously at the stem. But try as he would, he couldn't make the pretty little curls of smoke mount up into the air as he had watched his father and other men do. Very soon, however, a deathly sickness began to steal over him. His head and stomach hurt, and he could scarcely help falling down on the floor of the cellar.

"O Will," he said, as he gave the pipe to his cousin, "I am so sick! Let's get out of here. I feel as though I was going to die!" And John started in an attempt to find the opening through which he had entered the cellar, but to his surprise and terror he could not find it.

"O Will," he said, "this is all your fault! You know I didn't want to smoke. I wish now that I hadn't listened to you. Father said tobacco would make me sick, but I didn't know it would be so bad as this. Tell me, does it always make people sick? and do they ever die?"

"Yes, it usually makes them pretty sick," Will answered. "But they always get over it; and each time they smoke, they get more used to it, or something, and after a while they don't get sick at all. Look at me. It never makes me sick, but it did at first. Surely you can stand a little sickness when you know that it is going to make a man of you!"

John concluded that under those circumstances he could endure his suffering. But he did not try to smoke any more that morning. With Will's assistance he found the doorway of the cellar and went out where the air was more pure. Gradually, he began to feel better. When dinner time came, however, he did not care to eat; but he kept repeating to himself, "It won't be this way long, and I can afford to suffer if it will make a man of me." How sad to think that one so young should be so deceived!

Could someone have taught him then that the sick feeling that had so distressed him was caused by the strong poison contained in the tobacco, it might have encouraged him never to touch it again. Had his father explained that every pound of tobacco contains three hundred and twenty grains of this poison, one grain of which will kill a large dog in about three minutes; or told him the story of how a man once ran a needle and thread that had been dipped in the poison through the skin of a frog and of how the frog in a few moments began to act like a drunken person, vomited, and hopped about as fast as possible, and then laid down, twitched for a moment in agony, and died; or informed him that many people become insane just through the use of tobacco, John might have yet been influenced to leave the poisonous stuff alone—but perhaps his father did not know. Anyway, John was left without this much-needed information.

Boys who are not properly warned of the danger of tobacco-using are to be pitied more than blamed if they indulge; but their ignorance does not lessen the harm and the evils wrought. When the poison gets into the system, it affects the most vital organs; it undermines that strength and destroys that beauty which ornament true manhood and which assure an individual of success. Besides, the continued using causes the indulger to form a habit that cannot be easily overcome.

John, being not fully warned of the dreadful consequences of using tobacco, and yet determined to become a man, kept on smoking until he so accustomed his system to the shock that he felt satisfied he was becoming a conqueror and would soon be able to show his father that he was now a man.

During the time that John was undergoing such severe temptation, his father was very busy. He realized that his child needed more instruction than he was receiving and that Will's influence over John was not good; but just what advice to give, he hardly knew. Once he thought that he could smell tobacco smoke on his boy's clothing so calling John to his side, he said:

"John, I feel that I must tell you something more about certain bad habits that so many boys form while they are young. You remember I told you that smoking and chewing tobacco ruin many a life. Now, I am not going to say that you cannot use tobacco; but I wish that for my sake, as well as for your own, you would let it alone, for it is indeed a very bad habit."

To this advice John made no reply; for an appetite was being formed, and in his heart he decided to keep right on. It would have been better could his father have remembered the temptations of his own boyhood days. He might then have more fully realized how next to impossible it is for a parent to availingly teach his child to do something without first setting before the child an example that is worthy of imitation. Could he have helped his little son to understand the true meaning of manhood and the necessity of building up within himself in youth a noble, honest, and always-to-be-depended-upon character, as well as the need of developing a strong body, he might have laid a foundation upon which John could have later safely builded.

John dearly loved his father and wanted to please him. And to his mind he could best please his father by as quickly as possible becoming a man. So, with the thought of early manhood ever before him, he felt that, in using tobacco, he was doing right. And then, too, Charley had learned to smoke and chew, and it would be very hard indeed to be near the boys and not to join in with them.

By the time that John had passed his seventh birthday, the small amount of tobacco that was kept in the cellar was not sufficient to fill the demand of the three boys without too rapidly diminishing the uncle's supply, and the boys decided to look elsewhere.

Now, John's aunt had at one time explained to the boys

that lying and stealing are wrong; but she had not made it clear that deceiving is lying and that taking little things that did not belong to them, even though they took the things from some member of the family, is stealing, and that just such thefts lead to the greater crimes that send men and women to prison. Instead, she gave the advice in such a way that, though they were impressed with a horror of stealing, the boys could only in part comprehend her meaning. But because she had warned them, she felt that she had done her duty and that they ought to know right from wrong in regard to that matter without further explanation.

She did not realize that it was her duty to watch, encourage, and advise, and also to find out when mischief was being planned. In fact, this aunt and mother, busy with her own cares, knew nothing of the possibilities for a child whose confidence and love had been won, and who, through loving counsel, had gained a knowledge of evils and their effects before he had formed ruinous habits or his mind had been polluted with false ideas. Being thus left to themselves to discern as best they could the difference between right and wrong, the boys nearly always chose the wrong; and as a result, constantly went deeper and deeper into sinful things.

CHAPTER III
What the Big Chest Contained

Great sins always have a beginning; the first attempts to do evil are not hard to check if taken in time, but if allowed to be carried out, it is impossible to tell what the results may be. How sad it was that John and his cousins did not have someone to check them!

The boys now decided to keep close watch, and to avail themselves of every opportunity to procure tobacco, even if they were forced to steal it. The word "steal" had, of course, a certain horror to John because of the picture his aunt had described of a prison and a thief; but he soothed his conscience by saying, "There isn't anything else in the world except tobacco that I would think of stealing." But the stealing habit, like the tobacco habit, continues to grow stronger, unless it is in some way broken. As tobacco contains a poison that affects the physical being, so in a similar manner lying and stealing have a ruinous effect upon the moral nature. The three—lying, stealing, and tobacco using—too often go hand in hand.

The first effort of the boys to secure the much-coveted tobacco was made one day when they, while roaming about over the prairie, discovered a man hard at work in a field. The man seemed to be lifting something that was very heavy, and Will suggested to the boys that they go and lend their services provided the man would give them each a chew of his tobacco in return; and Will did not forget to add that they must each take as generous a bite as their mouths could accommodate. The man was glad to accept their help; and together with his own efforts, the work was soon finished. Then, in fulfillment of his agreement, he handed them his plug of tobacco that they might each take the "chew" he had promised them.

According to Will's suggestion the boys did not stop with an ordinary chew; but each took all that his mouth would contain. When they returned the plug, it was so small that the boys were all afraid the man would find fault with them; so they hurried away from the spot as rapidly as possible. As soon as they were far enough away, they removed the tobacco from their mouths; and they found that, by taking very small chews at a time, the amount was sufficient to last them for some time. Several times they succeeded in securing tobacco in this way, and by economizing were able to get along pretty well for a while. But the plan did not always work; for the neighbors' becoming aware of the scheme, prepared themselves with a small piece of tobacco to offer the greedy boys.

After that, in order to secure their tobacco, they were often forced to pick up partly-chewed quids, found where they had been thrown away by the owners. These the boys usually washed; sometimes, however, in their eagerness they could not wait to attend to even this amount of cleanliness, but crammed the tobacco into their mouths just as they had found it. Even cigar stubs; in fact, everything in the form of tobacco, that had been thrown away, they eagerly gathered and used to satisfy their ravenous appetites.

With a foundation now laid for both lying and stealing and with their consciences dulled, the boys were constantly laying plans to gratify their evil desires. Many a pocket they robbed of its contents if it happened to contain tobacco in any form. But this was a slow process at best; even under the most favorable circumstances it yielded them but very little returns for their efforts. But one day Will informed the boys that he had made a discovery—that he had found out that there was a lot of plug tobacco in the big chest in his father's room. "Now, if we could think up some way to get into that chest when the old folks are gone away to town," he suggested, "we could get all the chewing tobacco we would want for a long while. I thought I would watch and see where Dad put the key, but he took it with him. Guess he carries it with him everywhere he goes. I wonder if we couldn't manage in some way to break the lock. My, but I tell you we could get a big haul! I wonder if we hadn't better try it some day when the old folks go to town?"

"Hooray, that's just it!" shouted the smaller boys in the same breath.

And John asked quickly: "When will they go to town again? This is only Wednesday."

"It won't be long, I'm sure," Will answered reassuringly. "They'll go either Friday or Saturday sure. But we'll have to get busy and think out a way to break that lock. My, but won't the old man be mad when he finds out about it! We'll have to act just as if we couldn't see how on earth such a thing could have happened."

"Yes; and we'll have to hide the tobacco good, or Pa might find it," chimed in Charley.

"Hey, Will," John exclaimed in a hurried undertone—for all the boys had learned to speak low when mentioning their plans—"if we could take the hinges off from the back of the chest, we wouldn't have to break the lock at all."

"Why, John, that's just it! How in the world did you think of that scheme?" Will exclaimed, as he slapped his little cousin on the back. "I say, my boy, you had better look out or you'll be a man before your big cousin! It doesn't matter, you know, about the height, if you have the sense."

Now, John (although so young) was quite ingenious; and he often suggested ideas that, for their shrewdness, were far beyond his years. For such he was always praised by Will, and was encouraged to make other plans.

Being encouraged by his cousin's praise, the child's brain became even more active, and he said, "If we just cut a little piece from each plug, Uncle won't be so apt to miss the tobacco."

"That's just it again!" emphatically assented Will. "I declare, John, you surprise me! And now, we must have everything all ready so that the minute they leave we can get busy. Let's see, what'll we need? A screw-driver—and will we need a hammer?"

"We'll need a real sharp knife to cut the tobacco," John suggested.

"I'll get the things ready," Charley volunteered; and so they planned and waited for the time to come when they could carry out their scheme.

The time came on the following Saturday. Early in the morning the uncle and aunt drove away in the "buckboard," and were on their way to the city where they were to do their trading. All three of the boys had been unusually anxious to help their elders get started, forgetting in their eagerness that they might be thus revealing some of their plans. Scarcely did they give the uncle and aunt time to disappear in the distance before they had commenced their evil work.

"Here's the tools," Charley said, as he brought forth the screw-driver, hammer, and sharp knife. "Where shall I put them?"

"Oh, anywhere so they'll be handy!" Will told him; and then the three boys hastened to the room containing the chest and were soon kneeling on the floor, examining carefully the object of their interest.

The chest, a long, narrow, flat box somewhat darkened with age, was closed and securely fastened; and the tiny padlock that hung from its side seemed to say, "If you please, I am here to protect my master's property from the hand of any thieves; and to the extent that it is within my power, I shall perform my duty." Its bold front and defiant appearance did not, however, daunt the purpose of the boys. After giving it a brief examination, they slipped around to the opposite side of the chest, and by the aid of the screw-driver, removed the lower half of the rusty hinges.

"Thank goodness, this chest is old!" Will exclaimed as he brushed from his forehead the large beads of perspiration. "If these screws turned any harder, I never could get them out. Guess we'll earn our tobacco this time all right!"

Opening the Chest
Opening the Chest

Scarcely had the last screw been removed when up came the lid; and almost instantly three pairs of eager eyes were greedily gazing down upon the contents of the wooden chest. There were in it a package of old letters, various articles of clothing, a few trinkets, etc.; but only that part of the contents that was carefully packed in one corner claimed the attention of the boys. This, a pile of long brown strips, or plugs, of tobacco, was what they wanted; and soon Will was busily engaged in cutting a narrow slice from each plug and John and Charley were dividing the slices into three equal parts. But in their haste and excitement, none of the boys forgot to fill their mouths with the filthy stuff, and to chew while they worked.

As Will cut a piece from the last plug, he glanced about over the piles and said with a look of satisfaction: "Now that ain't so bad, is it, boys? That ought to last quite a spell; and when it's gone, we can come back here, or maybe something else will turn up." And then, when he saw the boys rearranging the tobacco in the chest, he said, "Look out there! You'll have to get everything just like it was, or we'll be caught and have had our fun for nothing!" When the chest was repacked, the last screw in its place, and the tiny scraps of tobacco that had fallen upon the floor had been carefully preserved, the boys looked at one another with satisfaction, and Will said, "That's a pretty slick job all right, if I do say so; and its a lot better than breaking the lock would have been. I'll tell you it takes some brains to do up a thing like that, and it makes me feel as if I'd like more of them."

To this John smiled and said: "Hey, Will, do you know what's in that trunk?" John referred to a large trunk that was sitting near the bed on the opposite side of the room.

"Couldn't tell you all that's in it, but it's locked; and it's in that trunk that Dad keeps his revolvers. There's two of them, because I saw inside the trunk the other day." And then as the new thought presented itself to his mind, he exclaimed, "I wonder why we couldn't get into that trunk the same as we did the chest?"

In a twinkling, all the boys were examining the trunk, but to their dismay, they found that the hinges, instead of being on the outside of the trunk, were arranged differently, and they could not get at them. Again it was John who suggested a plan whereby they could accomplish their desires. "Just take a nail," he said, "and turn the head of it around in the lock. I've watched my father do that, and he gets his open every time."

The trunk, which was an old one, yielded quickly to the efforts made by the boys; and upon raising the lid, they saw before them two shining weapons that were supposed to have been carefully hidden away from their inexperienced fingers. John and Will each quickly caught one up in his hand; and Will began handling his as though it were a toy, but not so did John.

John's father had taught him something of the dangers connected with the handling of a gun or revolver. Besides, John was at one time present when a duel was fought; and on that occasion one of the duelists was killed. The memory of that incident and of his father's warnings, made John very careful about pointing the revolver at either of his cousins. It was, therefore, with intense fear that John looked into the barrel of his cousin's revolver as Will snapped it, aimlessly pointing in his direction; and John exclaimed, "Turn that thing away, or you'll shoot me."

Will's answer was: "You needn't be afraid, John. This revolver isn't loaded."

But John, seeing his cousin's careless attitude, was afraid; and he dodged down behind a barrel of carpet-rags near which he had been standing. It was well that John did not longer remain where he had been; for the revolver contained a solitary load, and the frequent pulling of the trigger discharged this. The bullet passed the very spot where John had a moment before been standing, and lodged itself deep in the side of the trunk.

This experience marked an awakening-time in all of the boys' lives; at that moment their consciences, which had almost fallen asleep, were aroused, and in startling phrases gave them accounts of their evil deeds. With great haste the boys returned the weapons to their former hiding place, relocked the trunk, and in so far as it was possible, covered all the traces of the accident. Then, with hearts full of guilty thoughts, the three boys hastened from the place where a scene of horror had very nearly been enacted.

Out in the open, where the air was fresh and pure, their spirits to a certain degree revived. But their usual laughter, fun, and merry-making had been dampened; and as they wended their way to the prairie pasture-land, few words were passed between them. Poor little misguided boys! warned, and yet left so ignorant of what was the right and the wrong way.

Through the voice of conscience God endeavored to speak to John and to tell him that his ways were evil and that he and his cousins would some day get into serious trouble if they continued in the way they were going; but, although he was sad, he could not understand. He wanted to be a good boy for his father's sake (for his father was the best friend he knew); and most of all he desired to become the man that that parent had wished him to be. John's disregard for his father's warnings from time to time had been due to the fear that, if he obeyed, his early manhood would be hindered.

Could that father have given his little son an object-lesson such as an aged monk once, while walking through a forest, gave his scholar, John might have been spared much suffering. The monk, stepping before four plants that were close by, pointed to the first, a plant just beginning to peep above the ground; to the second, one well-rooted in the earth; to the third, a small shrub; and to the fourth, a full-sized tree.

Then turning to his young companion, he said, "Pull up the first." This the boy easily did.

"Now, pull up the second." The youth obeyed, but not with so much ease.

"And now the third." This time before the boy succeeded in uprooting the plant, he had to put forth all his strength and to use both his arms.

"And now," said his master, "try your hand on the fourth." But although the lad grasped the trunk of the tree in his arms, he scarcely shook its leaves; and he found it impossible to tear its roots from the earth. Then the wise old man explained the meaning of the four trials.

"This, my son," he said, "is just what happens to our bad habits and passions. When they are young and weak, we can by a little watchfulness and by a little discipline, easily tear them up; but if we let them cast their roots deep down into our souls, no human power can uproot them. Only the almighty hand of the Creator can pluck them out. For this reason, my boy, watch your first impulses."

Or, could John have heard the story of the giant who fell in with a company of pigmies, he might have taken a different course. The giant roared with laughter at the insignificant stature and wonderful boastings of the pigmies. He ridiculed their threats when they told what they expected to do to him; but when he fell asleep that night, he was at their mercy. And he did not know until he awoke in the morning that while he was asleep these tiny people of whom he had made sport had bound him with innumerable threads and that he was their helpless captive. But John knew nothing of these stories or of other things that teach the lessons he so much needed; and perhaps his father did not know, so that he could tell his son what he should have been told.

The use of tobacco is an evil. When God made tobacco and pronounced it good, He did not mean for it to go into the mouth of any man or woman, much less into the mouths of children. Tobacco is a deadly poison; and the constant use of any poison must injure the body of the one who uses it. When it has sapped the strength from both the mind and the body, it leaves the individual weakened in every way and makes it harder for him to live a good, pure life.

No person who uses tobacco may be said to be perfectly

well. Such a person may not realize how his health is impaired, because the stupor that the poison produces numbs his sensibilities; but the very appetite he has for tobacco is in itself a disease. In order for an habitual user to realize the harm that tobacco is doing to his health, he has simply to stop its use for a short time and watch the effect on his system.

Tobacco is not a food that God intended man to eat. In man's case it feeds only a craving that it has itself created. But the leaves of the tobacco plant do serve as food for the large, green worms that live and thrive in tobacco fields. Yes; tobacco is "very good" for the "creeping things" for which it was created; but it was not intended as food for man.

Could John and his cousins have understood all this when the next tobacco famine came to them, it seems that each would surely have resisted the temptation to stoop down, pick up a partly chewed quid of tobacco, cram it greedily into his watering mouth, and chew it as though it was the sweetest morsel he had ever tasted. But the boys did not know. They thought such things were manly.

CHAPTER IV
Early School Days

By the time John was eight years old, the evil influences with which he had been surrounded in his uncle's home were rapidly telling on him. To be sure, there was still the same pathetic expression in his deep, brown eyes, and now and then there could be observed in them a mischievous glance or a merry twinkle; but his general appearance was that of a sadly neglected child. Still the busy aunt took little notice either of him or of her own boys.

In his heart John was longing for someone to take an interest in him and to love him—someone to whom he could go with his boyish heartaches and from whom he could gain the sympathy for which his heart was craving. To be sure, his father was still kind, and sometimes John would imagine that he could even feel his father's love. At such times the boy would press closer to his parent, hoping that he would at least with his arm caress him; but his father did not understand. He could see only the outward roughness; and he said in his heart:

"It is all because he has never had a chance. He has grown up here on the prairie like a wild thing. He has never been to school, and I must send him at once."

With this purpose in his heart John's father decided to return with his child to the place that had once been his happy home. In making the change there were, of course, many things to take into consideration. But under the circumstances, to go seemed the best and proper thing to do. The sad events, he reasoned, were all in a lifetime; and he must make the best of them. The home would for a time seem desolate, he knew, but he thought that perhaps they could become used to it; anyway, his boy must be in school. The school terms would not be long (for only three or four months of each year were set apart for school purposes); but even these short terms would be better than none.

To John the change meant more. The five years that he had spent in the home of his uncle had made his cousins seem to him like brothers; but still, as he considered his father's plans, he thought, "Perhaps it may be all right." His aunt was very kind while John and his father were preparing to move; and the day they bade her good-by she said such sweet things that he wanted to throw his arms about her neck. To his mind it was the very way in which his own dear mother would have spoken had she been alive.

When all was ready for the departure, the aunt said: "John, here are the two little turkeys that you have liked so well all summer. You may take them with you. They will help you to forget that you are alone when your father is away at his work"; and she handed him a small covered basket. Then the wagon containing their few belongings moved away from the place that for nearly five years they had called their home.

As they wended their way along the thoroughfare, they saw men at work in the fields. Some were shucking corn and tossing the bright golden ears into wagons that were placed between the rows for that purpose, while others were hauling the grain to their barns to store it away for the winter's use. The broad corn leaves rustling in the wind seemed to whisper, "Winter is coming with his cold, bleak storms to rob the earth of her summer splendor; but he will bring his beautiful coverlet of snow to protect her fields and to prepare them for the coming year."

The foliage on the small bushes that were scattered here and there was fading; but the air was still soft and mild. Near the willows might still be seen the bending goldenrods, asters, and sunflowers. And occasionally blue smoke could be seen curling up from some sod-house chimney.

It was evening when the father and his son drove up to the door of their long-desolate home; the sun was sinking lower and lower in the west. A few soft glimmers of its mellow light lingered timidly about the doorway as if to bid the home-comers welcome, and then they were gone. A rabbit, hopping boldly about in the neglected doorway, stopped suddenly as if to ask why these people had come to a place that she had chosen for her home; and some prairie dogs that had formed a colony close by anxiously watched from the entrance of their underground homes to see what was going on.

John and his father, each absorbed with his own thoughts, sprang from the wagon, and soon began to air out the musty house and to rearrange the furniture that had long been idly awaiting their return. After a while John found that his aunt had not forgotten that he would be very hungry, and soon he was sampling some large bread-and-meat sandwiches; his father, too, came for his share. Thus quickly passed the first evening in their old home. But before John retired to his own bed, he saw that his little turkeys received some attention; and in the morning he let them have their freedom.

As the days sped by and lengthened into weeks and months, John would have indeed been lonely had it not been for his little pets, the turkeys. They received his earliest attention in the morning, and it was their little beaks that touched his cheek the last thing before he retired at night; and to himself alone was their roosting-place known.

How different everything seemed to John in his new home! The change from knowing nothing but perfect freedom in God's great open out-of-doors to being left alone to hustle off to school in the early morning hours, where he must sit like a statue and prepare humdrum lessons, was to John a wonderful change. John, however, was determined to make the very best of his lot and to do all that he could to please his teacher.

Allowing this purpose to govern his life, John's conduct was such that he became in a very short time the favorite pupil in the school; and his kindly, generous, and ambitious nature won him many friends. He was soon noted for his witty remarks, made in a manner so droll and unpretentious that often merry bursts of laughter were heard from his teacher as well as his playmates.

But regardless of these pleasant conditions, John was far

from happy. He still wanted someone to show deep love for him and to take an interest in his welfare; and though he constantly tried to smother the deep suffering he felt it still smoldered in his heart. This, perhaps, caused him to crave all the more tobacco that in a way had dulled his senses and caused him to realize his troubles less.

CHAPTER V

The Card Parties

While John was forming new acquaintances at school, Satan was not asleep. John's active mind was soon being schooled in many evils that he had not known before. And to make the matter still worse, John's father had a number of bachelor friends with whom he was in the habit of meeting for pleasant evenings, and their amusements were mostly drinking strong drinks and playing card games.

Among these men, as among his schoolmates, John became a favorite; and he was often praised and admired for his shrewd and manly ways. And when the report concerning his intense desire to become a man was circulated among them, they urged him to drink beer, saying that it would make him more manly and that all men must learn how to drink and smoke if they would be thought of as being manly. As a result John was soon able to drink his share of the beer, although he did not like the taste at first. Besides this, John discovered that at these evening gatherings he could often replenish his supply of tobacco by slipping a little from someone's pocket when the owner was not on his guard.

Poor little John!—such a favorite! so gifted, and yet so neglected! in regard to high ideals and purposes in life, so ignorant! and so desirous of that motherly love and interest that were ever denied him! He endeavored to fill his life with other things; but in his day-dreams he often pictured his mother, and wondered: "Was she like my aunt? Would she take me and hold me in her arms while she smoothed my hair with her hand? Would she bind my bruises? And would she sit by my bedside at night and hold my hand in hers while telling me stories that she had read?" "Oh, how would it all seem?" he would ask himself; and then, remembering that such could never be, he would try to forget and be happy. His mother was gone, he reasoned, and he must be content. It was to his two little feathered friends alone that he confided his sorrows.

Had John's father remembered the determination that filled his soul on the dark day of his wife's funeral, and had he continued to teach his little son to pray and to serve God, how much better it might have been! How much better might John have understood the difference between right and wrong! In such a case, John's life's record might have been filled with good and noble deeds, and his habits might have been clean and wholesome.

As it was, because of his ignorance of right, he was laying a crumbling foundation formed of evil motives and desires. And should he continue to build, using similar material, his life's structure would be unsafe; it would be momentarily in danger of falling. As Satan is ever waiting with the needed supplies for a work of this kind, so he was ready to aid little John. The card parties at which John and his father were often present furnished John with much of his material.

The younger men among those who attended these gatherings, recognizing in John material of the entertaining sort, began at once to educate him. They taught him, not only to drink beer, but also to play cards and to swear. To John beer did not at first have a pleasant taste; but as it was when he was trying to learn to use tobacco, so it was now—the promise that it would help him in becoming manly encouraged him to take more; and as he drank, the appetite grew. Finally, he would sometimes drink so much that he could not keep awake.

Usually on these occasions beer was served only as a prize to the winners of the games. The lucky fellow alone was given a drink while those who had lost were given only a smell of the bottle. One time when John had won in a number of games and had been treated to as many drinks from the bottle of beer, he became very sleepy. Going over to one corner of the room, he crept up on a table and soon was apparently asleep. It happened, however, that, although he was sleepy, he was not wholly unconscious to what was going on; and suddenly he heard a plot that seemed to him so cruel that he could scarcely believe his ears.

A Card-Party
A Card-Party

At the close of such gatherings, a chicken-roast was generally in order, and the fowl used was usually taken from some hen-roost not far distant. On this particular occasion when the party was about to break up, John heard the roughest of the company ask:

"I say, boys, who's goin' fer the roast tonight? Some one ought to be off fer it's nigh onter the midnight hour, and I, fer one's got a big job ahead a me tomorrer."

"I'll go, Bill," someone answered; "but wha do ye say ter go?"

"Oh, it don't make no difference, so's it's not too fer away!" the other answered, and added: "Whist, Tom, why can't we git John's turkeys? They'd make fust-rate eatin' all right. He's too far gone to know anything about it."

John was just about to call out that they must let his turkeys alone when he remembered how hard it would be in the darkness to discover their roosting-place, so he remained quiet. It was, however, with some uneasiness that he awaited the thieves' return. When they came, he was relieved; for they were carrying chickens instead of turkeys. Although, because of the safety of his pets, a thrill of satisfaction swept over John, yet he had received in his heart a wound that was deep and wide. These cruel, heartless men were willing to take from him, in so unprincipled a manner, his only companions and playfellows. John somewhat realized that life had a hard and bitter side for him; but again he endeavored with all his strength to make the best of it.

It was morning before John and his father returned to their home; and it was with unusual joy that John found his pets waiting for their breakfast. As he held them close to his breast, with their beaks close to his cheek, he again thought of his mother; also he wondered about a certain change that had come over his father.

For a time after their removal to their own home, the father had been very devoted to John and had seemed to understand something of the boy's loneliness. Perhaps it was a realization of this loneliness and a desire to bring into the life of the child the motherly interest of which he had been deprived that had turned the father's heart toward a certain young lady of his acquaintance. Anyway, whatever was the cause, the father became more and more interested in this young woman; while, on the other hand, he paid less attention to John, whose loneliness daily increased. Night after night John's pillow was dampened by the tears he shed while waiting and listening for the sound of his father's returning footsteps.

In course of time the father married and brought home his new bride. At first John was very shy; but he was glad. Oh, how he wished that she would be what he had day-dreamed that his own mother might have been! He could then have given her all his love and confidence. He could have told her all his boyish plans for the future, asking her for the advice he would need. But the new mother failed to fulfill his hopes. Even she did not understand the longings of his boyish heart; nor did she realize that the poor little neglected boy was measuring her by what he had imagined a true mother to be. She was kind to John; but that was all. Her time and attention were given to her husband; and John daily saw the gulf between his father and himself widening and deepening. A feeling of discord crept into John's heart; all attraction for home was severed; and he felt that his happiness would have to be sought from other sources.

CHAPTER VI
Visitors and Pastimes

During the winter that followed his father's marriage, John's stepmother's brother came to live with the family; and the influence of this stepuncle, whose name was Ed, was as bad or worse than Will's or Charley's could ever have been; for Ed was older and wiser, and knew much more of sin.

In Ed's home both the father and the mother used tobacco a long time before their child was born. When he was just a little infant, he worried and cried a great deal. He continued to do this, seemingly never to be satisfied, until finally the parents imagined that he wanted tobacco; and sure enough he did. The mother tied a small amount in a rag and gave it to her baby to suck, and immediately he became quiet and contented. So, from that time she gave him tobacco to stop his crying. As he grew, the quantity he used gradually increased until, when he was in his teens, he spent much of his money for tobacco. He went without many of the necessary things of life in order that he might have the money those things would cost to spend for tobacco.

The Bible tells us that God is abundant in goodness and truth, keeping mercy for thousands and forgiving iniquity and transgression and sin ... Parents may be sorry for their sins, and be forgiven for their transgressions; but their children must suffer from inherited ill-dispositions, unnatural appetites, or diseases.... Oh, what a responsibility is resting upon the parents of the future generations!

Now, tobacco acts directly on the mind. It clouds the understanding and dulls the memory; and sometimes it has much worse effects. The story is told of the experience of a brilliant young man—a graduate from Andover College—who, for a time, seemed to have a wonderful future before him. After a few short successful years, however, all hopes were blighted; he was thrown into an insane asylum a physical wreck. The doctors said that tobacco had done it; but regardless of this, he was each day given, according to the rules of the asylum, a small quantity of tobacco. For twenty years he was in this seemingly hopeless condition; and then suddenly, one day as he was walking the floor, his reason returned, and he realized what was the matter. Throwing the plug of tobacco through the iron grate of his cell, he said: "What brought me here? What keeps me here? Why am I here? Tobacco! tobacco! tobacco! God help, help! I will never use it again!"

He was restored; and for ten years he preached the gospel.

But not only does tobacco injure the mind; it also affects the blood and sensitive tissues and the different organs of the body, which in order to act normally and to do their work properly must be in healthful condition. When the blood becomes saturated with the deadly poison that comes from the pipe or cigar, and the soft membranes of the mouth become filled with the poisonous secretion from the quid, as a consequence, every member of the body becomes affected, and disease and suffering are the final results. Lord Bacon said, "To smoke is a secret delight, serving to steal away men's brains." Many others have expressed themselves in even louder terms against the evil effects of tobacco; but we must now return to John and to Ed, his stepuncle.

Soon after Ed came to live in the family, he paid a visit to a neighboring town; and while there, he stole from a store a case of plug tobacco. This he stealthily brought to his sister's new home, confiding his secret to no one except John; and by generous promises he persuaded John to say nothing about the matter. At this time John was in his thirteenth year. He still keenly felt that something was dreadfully missing in his life; so he turned to Ed, hoping to find that something in his companionship. But again he was disappointed. The standard of Ed's ideals were so far below the standard that John had fixed for himself that John was conscious of a constant repulsion in his heart toward Ed. As a consequence, John's loneliness increased.

About the time Ed arrived in the neighborhood, another

dangerous pastime was introduced. Dancing found a place in the social gatherings; and again John was an apt scholar. Before very long he was considered to be one of the best among the young people in this art; and for the time being he seemed to find real enjoyment in the amusement. There was a fascination about it that helped him partly to forget his troubles and heartaches, also the discouragements with which he had been haunted so much of late.

During the winter that followed, the social spirit increased and the months were full of changes and excitement. The uncle with whom John and his father had spent several years came with his family for a prolonged visit. A hearty welcome was given the visitors, especially by John; for regardless of the fact that in order to make room for the company he had to exchange his nice warm bed in the house for a less comfortable one in the sod cellar, he rejoiced in the thought that he could once more be with his old companion, Will. In fact, any change was appreciated by John in his restless, discontented frame of mind.

The first evening the boys retired early, partly because they had no light and partly because they wanted to visit about bygone days. They had so many things to say to each other; and besides, they wanted to lay their plans for a jolly time while they could be together. Will laughed heartily about John's intense desire to become a man, and asked him how he felt about it now. It was in a discouraged tone of voice that John replied:

"There ain't so much fun in it as I supposed. The older I get, the more unhappy I feel. Why, Will, there are times when I almost wish that I were dead. No one seems to care for me or to have any time to give me. It's just 'John here' and 'John there'; and if I dare to say anything, I'm laughed at or told to keep still. It was different before Pa got married. Then he used to talk to me and try to help me when I got lonesome; but now I just have to get along the best way I can. If I like anything it's all right, and if I don't it's the same.

"I'll just tell you, if it wasn't for Pa, I'd run away from home! As for being a man, I don't think that it is so wonderful after all. The men that I know are all so bad. Just look at Ed! I'm getting so that I can hardly endure Ed!"

In reply to John's great outburst of sorrow, Will had no words of sympathy to offer. All that he could propose was that they could spend their evenings in playing cards (for Will, too, had learned many things since John had left; and card-playing was one of them). John was pleased with the suggestion; but he said, "I haven't any cards." As usual, however, he was quick to invent a way out of that difficulty and added: "Hey, Will! why couldn't we make some? I know where there's a lot of cardboard boxes that we could cut up. One could cut while the other marked them. You would know how to make them, would you not?"

"Yes, I think so," Will answered. "We could do that all right in the daytime; but how could we work in the dark? And does it get very cold in here?"

"Oh, it doesn't get so awfully cold; and as for a light, I can get a dish of lard and put a rag in it which we can light! That won't be a very good light; but I think we can get along."

The boys found that it was no small task to make the cards. First they had to cut the cardboard. This John did with a very sharp knife. Next, they drew hearts and diamonds and other necessary markings. To be sure, the set of cards was a very crude one when it was finished; and when the boys began to shuffle them in the pack, they were disappointed because of the bulky appearance and wished for a more perfect set. But John had done a good job in cutting them out, and the marking answered the purpose very well. So night after night, by the aid of the flickering and sputtering light, furnished by the rag burning in the saucer of lard, the two boys, with heads bent low, sat scheming and planning, each striving to get ahead of the other in the game.

Long before Will's visit was ended, both boys had

become so skillful in playing that the one could scarcely get the better of the other unless one in some way cheated. This caused them to try many underhanded tricks and encouraged them to bet and gamble; and in course of time they had exchanged as wagers the greater part of their simple belongings. Taking advantage of one another became a part of the game and seemingly was the principal aim. And the evenings that they did not spend in dancing were spent in indulging in these dangerous amusements. (Card-playing—as does also dancing—wields an influence that is very harmful, especially to the young. As the interest in the game increases, the players' desire for things that are good and wholesome is lessened. One player sees only the pleasure that he derives from getting the better of the one he is playing against. He fails to see that each time he stoops to unfair methods in order to gain his purpose he helps to pave the way for other things that are wrong and deceitful.)

When the first warm days of spring arrived and the grass of the prairie began to unfold its tiny blades, John's uncle said it was time for him and his family to return home. "It's a long way, Will," he said; "and we must get there in good time to plant a big crop of 'tobaker.' You remember we didn't have near enough to do us last year!" Will agreed; but the boys were all sorry to be separated again, and when the day of departure came, it was very hard indeed for them to bid one another farewell.

During the winter months John had not thought much about his aunt, for Will and he had been too deeply interested in other things. But now at the last moment that old longing again clutched at his heart. When he saw them disappearing in the distance and finally lost them to view, like a flash the desire that had so long been smoldering within his heart was fanned, as it were, into a mighty flame, and in his mind he resolved what he would do. "I will stay in this home no longer!" he cried in his distress. "My father may miss me; but if I stay here, I shall die!" and going to his father, he stated his intentions.

CHAPTER VII
Leaving Home

As John's father looked into the deep pathetic eyes of his son, he in part understood the meaning of what he read. He could see that the soul of his child was crying out for something; but again he failed to understand the true longings of the young heart. He failed to see that the boy was being crushed by sinful habits, and that for parental care and interest he was starving. In ignorance the father supposed that the boy's unrest was due to a longing to know more of the world, to a feeling akin to that which an explorer experiences.

Poor man! Could he have known just then what really was troubling his boy, he could have stayed the spirit of unrest by holding out to John the "olive branch of peace." He could have said: "John, we have drifted apart. We are not to one another what we used to be. Stop, my boy; sit down here. Let us carefully talk these things over before you take such a step. Out in the world you will meet many temptations and evils, more than you have ever known." And many other tender words of advice he might have spoken to the child; but these things were left unspoken.

Instead, his father only said, "John, I would like to have you remain at home a while longer; but if you are determined to go, you may, only remember to try to do as nearly right as you can! I have wanted to bring you up well for your mother's sake; for she had made so many plans for your future. My wish, John, is that you become a good man."

John was deeply touched by his father's farewell speech; and had there been any other drawing to keep him at home, he certainly would have remained. As it was, he soon gathered together his belongings, and while still in his thirteenth year, said good-by to his people, and went away to work for a thrifty farmer.

During the two years preceding his departure from home, John had now and then worked for the farmers in different parts of the country. This and his attendance at the social gatherings had enabled him to become acquainted with numbers of boys, some of whom were very wild and rough. But because of the companionship of Will during the winter months, the evil influences of his wide circle of friends had not been so strong. But when the cousins were parted, John's companions were again some of the roughest and toughest in the community. Because of this his tobacco and beer bills increased, and to this alarming expenditure he added many accounts for whiskey.

John had made a discovery. He had found that Ed, in order to satisfy the awful craving and gnawing in his stomach (a sensation produced by the tobacco poison), was using a generous supply of whiskey; and for the same reason John began to use it. Whiskey did perhaps satisfy for the time being; but John also discovered that the seemingly good effect was very soon gone and that the old trouble was again there, only with renewed force and strength. Another thing he found, too, was that he had added to his list of evil habits one even more fierce and strong than the others.

When John left home, his desire was principally to find relief for his loneliness; but he had another object. His expenses had been heavy and hard to defray. And now with the amount he had to pay for his whiskey added to what he was already spending for beer and tobacco, his bills were so high he felt that he must have more money in order to meet them. This seeming necessity was, therefore, one thing that urged him to take the step he took.

Leaving the Old Homestead
Leaving the Old Homestead
The farmer for whom John began to work was known among his men as "the captain." All the hired help worked under one manager, or boss; so John's experience while in this service was new and varied.

"We have orders today to work for Farmer Z," explained

the boss one morning a few weeks after John's arrival. "And the captain says we must be sure and get around there early in the morning, for we are to get our breakfast over there."

The home of Farmer Z was some distance from that of John's employer; but the prancing horses on which the men were to ride were soon carrying them across the prairie, and it was not long until they were in sight of Farmer Z's modest farmhouse. As they entered the gateway, Farmer Z stepped into the doorway; and when he greeted the men with a kindly "Good morning," John particularly noticed his countenance and expression and wondered why he was so different from the comrades with whom he had always associated. He noticed, too, that, as the men gathered in the dining room and took their places around the table, they were quiet and reserved; and he was puzzled by still another thing—Farmer Z bowed his head and thanked God for all of His blessings and benefits and goodness to them all.

Such things were new and strange to John; and when at the close of the meal, the farmer invited them into another room, saying, "We always have reading and prayer immediately after breakfast and would be glad to have you all join with us," John suddenly felt extremely awkward and out of place, and he longed to make his escape to the barn.

John could have given no reason for his feelings, unless it was that the farmer's suggestion of prayer made him think about his mother and of the time when his father had taught him the little prayer, "Now I lay me down to sleep," and had told him that he very much desired him to be a little man. But it was not strange that John should feel as he did; for he had so often associated other scenes with that of learning the prayer, but had since that time heard very little about the Bible. In fact, the only part of the Bible that he had ever read was a few verses in the small New Testament that had belonged to his mother; and he had read these because he had heard that the reading of certain passages would stop the toothache and relieve the nosebleed. He experimented one time when he had the nosebleed, and his nosebleed did stop; but he was not sure that it would not have stopped as soon had he not read the verses.

Now, for some reason unknown to himself, John did not want to remain for worship; so when he noticed one of the other men slipping out of the back door, he quickly followed. The two were just about to enter the barn when the farmer, calling to them in words that were gentle but firm, said, "We always have our help come in with us for worship." Seeing then that there was no way around going in except to stoutly refuse, the two returned to the house; and with the others they seated themselves in the room where it was evident that the family worship was to be held. This experience was so entirely new to John that he actually suffered. He did not know what to do nor how to act.

He observed that the children, the workmen, and the farmer's wife, were all seated, so he sat down, too. He also observed that the men had left their hats outside where they had washed; and this caused him to feel very strangely, because he had his own in his hand. He dropped it, however, beside his chair; then he began to watch the children and to try to do just as they were doing. But as no two of the youngsters were doing the same thing, he again felt troubled. The older members of the family, he noticed, sat very still; and suddenly John realized that they must be listening to the farmer, who had been reading. John knew that he had not heard one single word that had been read, and here, the farmer was now saying, "Let us pray."

When they knelt beside their chairs, John was again bewildered; but having decided to do just as nearly as he possibly could the way the rest did, he, too, slipped down upon his knees. For some reason that he could not understand, a burning shame that seemed to benumb his whole being swept over him, and he could hardly hear the farmer's words; but he realized suddenly that the farmer was saying, "Dear Lord, bless the help today, and keep them from accidents and danger."

Hurriedly glancing around, John saw the children peeking

from between their fingers; and hastily covering his own face with his hands, he gave a quick glance toward Mr. A, his boss. Mr. A was kneeling beside his chair, but was picking his teeth and looking out of the window. Just then the farmer said, "Amen," and they all arose.

Then, as John compared his own attitude with that of Mr. A.'s, another feeling of shame came over him; and for some time he kept asking himself, "Why didn't I act unconcerned like the boss?" But John was not a bad boy naturally. He was ignorant of what was right. He had never understood that there is a Savior and that that Savior loved him and left an example for him to follow. To be sure, he had often heard both his Savior's and his Creator's names reviled and abused by his evil companions. But he did not know that these were Beings to whom he could go when in trouble; nor did he understand that in God's sight he was a sinner.

More than once that day while working, John thought of the farmer's words and wondered if the prayer would have any effect upon the day. Some way he thought it would, and he decided to watch and see. The day was ideal, and the help orderly; and God kept them free from accident and trouble. It was all a mystery to John, and he pondered over it along the way home and even during the night. Farmer Z had opened up a new channel for his thoughts.

CHAPTER VIII
With the Circus

During the following year a circus that was passing through the country stopped at a town near by; and John, together with a number of his associates, attended some of the exhibitions. John's interest was at once captivated, and he felt that it would be great to join the company and to act the part of the clown; and he soon began to plan to secretly join them the following season. His visions of great wealth enlarged day by day, and in fancy he pictured a future of wonderful fame.

In due time the show company returned. They gladly accepted John's proposal to join them; and so John, with his few earthly possessions, to the surprise of all who knew him, disappeared from his home locality. But John seemed doomed to disappointment; the showman's life was not at all as he had pictured it. Instead of becoming fabulously rich in a fairy-like way, he was taken very ill and had soon lost all the money he did have. As soon, therefore, as he was able, he returned to his friends at home, thoroughly disgusted with his undertakings; he was a wiser lad than he was when he went away.

But, although John was disgusted, he was not disheartened. When he was laughed at by his friends, he bravely bore their ridicule, and endeavored to look on the bright side of things. Also, he explained to them that show life, on the outside and to the sightseer, was not at all what it was among the members of the company; but that behind the curtains oaths were uttered, and abuse and nearly every kind of evils could be witnessed.

When he was back once more among his old associates, he endeavored to pass away the time in as pleasant a way as possible. Card playing, gambling, and dancing were his amusements, but tobacco and whiskey were his enjoyments; and as before, he was considered among his friends as a jolly good fellow. But John was not truly happy; beneath his superficial joyousness was a longing for something that he was unable to name or describe.

Let us stop a moment and look at John. A glance tells us that a great change has taken place. The ruddy complexion and childish features were replaced by a sallow hue upon the sunken cheek; and the roguish expression of the large brown eyes was lost in the haggard look that well accorded with the telltale cough and the stooping shoulders. The poisons of the tobacco and whiskey were doing their fatal work. His entire system was heavily charged with nicotine and alcohol; and the effect of these poisons constantly operating upon his nervous system and digestive organs had made him but a wreck of his former self. It is true that in stature he was as large as the man his father had desired him to be; but he was far from being of the strong manly type that that parent would have had him to become. Instead, he was weakly; and his body was never free from pain and suffering.

The old adage that ignorance is bliss can never be aptly applied to nicotine and alcohol. For only those who let them both entirely alone can be truly happy or safe. When we examine what doctors have written about the use of these poisons, we find that alcohol as well as nicotine is a stimulant and a narcotic. As a stimulant, it excites the brain and nerves, quickens the circulation of the blood, and intoxicates (makes drunk); while as a narcotic it blunts the powers of the brain and nerves and produces stupor and death.

Tests in the army, navy, and arctic explorations have definitely proved that alcohol is not a food.

Alcohol will not allay thirst: "Alcohol has a great attraction for water; and when swallowed, it draws the water to itself, thus depriving the tissues of the body of that merit necessary inorganic food. Again, alcohol causes a rush of blood to the skin, which causes a sensation of warmth to be felt upon the surface of the body. However, the sensation of heat is, like beauty, 'only skin deep,' as the heat of the system has really been diminished rather than increased; because when the blood is upon the surface, it parts with its heat more readily."

I "The effects of alcohol upon the heart may be summed up in the following statements:

"(a) It causes a softening of the muscles of the heart, and a fatty degeneration, thus clogging the workings of this vital organ.

"(b) It overworks the heart.

"(c) Oftentimes it renders the heart weak and flabby.

"(d) It causes an enlargement or dilation of its parts.

"(e) There is a consequent effect of drowsiness and lassitude.

"(f) Its general effect upon the heart is to destroy its strength and usefulness."

II "Alcohol has the following effects upon the lungs:

"(a) It makes the blood impure, thus increasing the work of the lungs.

"(b) It paralyzes the blood vessels.

"(c) It weakens the various lung tissues.

"(d) It impairs breathing."

III "Alcohol's effects upon the stomach:

"(a) Produces chronic inflammation of the stomach.

"(b) Injures the mucous lining by hardening the tissues.

"(c) It destroys some of the small glands and impairs others.

"(d) It precipitates the pepsin of the gastric juice, thus retarding digestion.

"(e) It thickens the mucus of the stomach.

"(f) The action of the stomach is at first quickened by the presence of alcohol, and then retarded."

IV "The effects of alcohol upon the liver may be:

"(a) It produces a hardened condition of its tissues.

"(b) Enlarges the organ.

"(c) Compresses and lessens the cells for producing bile.

"(d) Stimulates the liver to overaction, thus reducing the bile supply.

"(e) It weakens and destroys the usefulness of this organ of digestion."

V "Effect of alcohol upon the blood and blood-vessels:

"(a) It thins and coagulates the blood according to the amount of alcohol.

"(b) It hastens the circulation, thus weakening it.

"(c) It prevents combustion.

"(d) It impairs and destroys the corpuscles, thus affecting their powers of transporting oxygen and carbonic acid gas.

"(e) It weakens the arterial muscles by affecting the nerves governing them."

VI "Effects of alcohol upon the brain and nerves are:

"(a) It causes apoplexy and epilepsy by confusing the brain.

"(b) It weakens the will and deadens the feelings.

"(c) It hardens the brain tissues, producing dullness, insensibility, and insanity.

"(d) It destroys the nerve fiber of the brain.

"(e) It temporarily stimulates and finally depresses this organ.

"(f) It will at last destroy man, body and soul."

"Alcohol leads every other drug in its far-reaching influence for mischief and evil. Were the thousands of ruined homes, the untold numbers of blasted lives, the sorrows, the sins, numberless crimes, murders, and deaths brought in panoramic review before us, what a hell-born picture it would be!"

"The effect of alcohol upon the morals is awful. All delicacy, courtesy, and self-respect are gone; the sense of justice and right is faint or quite extinct. There is no vice into which the victim of drunkenness does not easily slide; and no crime from which he can be expected to refrain. Between this condition and insanity there is but a single step."

These are only a part of the many evils that come to the one who takes alcohol into his system. We have already heard something about the effects of nicotine, the poison that is in tobacco. The constant use of either poison will impair the health of the strongest person. It saps the mind of its reasoning qualities; and in nine cases out of ten, leaves the victim without sufficient strength to seek and obtain his own deliverance or to live a righteous life. But let us return now to John.

CHAPTER IX
Caught Unawares

At the age of eighteen John had come almost to the point of discouragement. His health was so poor that he did not know a well moment; and besides, his longing soul was still unsatisfied. He had always desired to be good and kind to all; but he did not know how to rise to a nobler plane of conduct than that on which he was living. He judged men by their moral conduct, and not by their spiritual life. In fact, he had very little, if any, comprehension of Christianity. He knew of a few, like Farmer Z., who professed religion; but he was afraid of these and he avoided their company.

He had now and then, with a number of other boys about his own age, visited some places where religious services were being held. But their object in going was to have a good time; and they seldom remained long enough to derive any good. On one of these occasions they went to a small school house that was located a few miles from the town of C. The meeting had been widely advertised, and a goodly number were in attendance; and when John and his companions had taken their seats well to the rear, there was only standing-room left. Curiosity was pictured on every face; for the ministers (one elderly, the other young) were two modestly dressed women, and lady preachers had never been heard of in that part of the country.

The singing was beautiful! John thought that the songs were sweeter than any he had ever heard. When prayer was being offered, he listened carefully to every word; and when he heard the ministers address God as their Father, asking Him to direct them in all that they did and said, and to prepare the hearts of the people to receive the truths that they were about to speak, he was instantly filled with wonder and awe.

After they rose from prayer, another song was sung; and then the elderly lady began to address the people. As she read in a clear, sweet voice a chapter from the Scriptures, John listened carefully. The account of the woes pronounced upon the people who would not do right and the promises made to those who would live right and were prepared to die, were truly wonderful. Especially was he impressed with one verse she read, though he realized very little of what it meant: "Therefore be ye also ready: for in such an hour as ye think not, the Son of man cometh."

When this speaker took her seat, the other lady, a young, sweet-faced girl, arose, and said a few words. After telling of how she had been converted, and of how the Savior had ever since supplied all the longings of her heart and had enabled her by his grace to live a life that was pure and spotless, she spoke of her home in heaven; and then she told the people that God would do the same for others as He had for her—for everyone who would give up evil habits and forsake sin, and who would love His Son, whom He had sent to the earth to suffer and die that all people might be saved. John listened to every word; and as the girl sat down, he thought, "Why, I would give everything that I have in the world to be able to say such things about myself!"

When making the announcements, the elderly lady said: "This meeting will be continued for three weeks or more, and we want as many of you as can to attend regularly; for there will be many portions of the Bible explained, and we want everyone to learn what is the road to success and to find out how to be truly happy." John at once decided that he would attend every service; but since at the same time he felt an interest similar to that which had inspired him to become a showman, he remembered that bitter experience and ground his teeth. He was about to change his decision to attend the meetings regularly, when he remembered the words, "Therefore be ye also ready; for in such an hour as ye think not, the Son of man cometh!"

Instantly he beheld a great panoramic view of his past life, and many of the evils that had never before appeared to him as sin were painted with the blackest dyes. He had not meant to be wicked, but he suddenly realized that his life had been wasted; and he concluded that he was not ready to meet Christ. But John believed that Christ would come to the earth, and he felt that he would give anything to be ready to meet Him.

As John, whenever he was perplexed or troubled, had been in the habit of doing, he reached down into his pocket and drew out a large plug of tobacco and began biting off a piece to chew. But what was the matter? The tobacco did not taste as it had in the past and it appealed to him so differently. It was now actually disgusting and repulsive to him; and he thought: "What a filthy habit! And to think of the time and money that it has cost me! Why have I been so foolish?"

The next instant he resolved that he would never again taste the horrid stuff. And very soon a few scenes of things that happened when he was under the influence of whisky came to his mind, and he shuddered. Never again would he touch that stuff, he determined. In fact, the greater part of the night John spent in reviewing his life; and he found that the larger portion of the things he had been doing were things he would not want to be found doing at the Savior's coming.

The following day John could hardly wait until the time came when he could again return to the little brown school house to hear more of the beautiful story that had so charmed him. And night after night found John in one of the seats in the rear of the building. It was not long until he discovered the pathway to heaven; he saw it bathed with heaven's sunshine and could see that it was for him to walk upon. But the next thing was for him to make the start.

It is one thing to decide that a certain thing is right and quite another thing to take a stand (regardless of what anyone may think or say) for the right. He had heard the preachers telling about the life of a Christian, the Savior's love and death, and God's great mercy, night after night for two weeks; but no invitation to come forward had been given to those desiring to make a change in their manner of living. The ministers desired that each one be given a full understanding of God's plan of salvation so that none would take a step in the dark.

John was fully decided to change his manner of living; but he did not want to make any more mistakes. For this reason he restrained himself from going to the motherly lady to inquire of her what he had better do. His old desire to become a man had revived, but this time he desired to be a man after God's own heart—pure and holy—like the one that God created in the beginning.

The time for an invitation to be given to the penitent finally came. Upon entering the meeting house that evening John noticed a slight change in the arrangement of the seats. The long row of chairs supplied by kind-hearted neighbors to help in seating the people had been removed, and a long, narrow bench had been put in their place. John wondered at the change, but did not have to wonder long. An announcement was soon made, stating that the bench was to serve as an altar, where those who desired to be converted and who wanted to consecrate their lives and services to God could gather for prayer.

An explanation was also made to the effect that, though God is pleased to see people humble themselves before Him, there was no virtue in the wooden altar; it was simply a more convenient place to bow for prayer than their seats would be. The services were shorter than usual; and when the invitation to come forward was given to those who desired to yield their hearts to God, John was ready. He longed to go; but although he had learned a great many things, he was still uncertain just what was meant by bowing at the altar; and as he wanted to do the right thing, he decided to wait until he saw how the others would do. He did not have long to wait; for a girl in front of him arose, went forward, and knelt down beside the altar. This was enough for John, because it taught him just what he desired to know; and he was soon kneeling beside her. That night was indeed a wonderful time. One by one the people flocked to the front part of the room; and John afterwards learned that many of his friends and even those whom he thought would ridicule and make fun of him, were among the number that, as himself, had sought and found pardon for their sins.

The invitation lasted a long time; and when it was ended, the ministers knelt down among the penitent seekers, thanked God for the tender mercies he had extended to the lost world, and prayed that those who were at the altar might understand what true salvation is. After praying, they explained carefully what it meant to be redeemed from all sin, and told the seekers how God looked upon the sin-cursed world and its awful wickedness, but also how He was so moved with tender love and compassion that He sacrificed the brightest Gem of glory—even His only begotten Son—to be a Redeemer for all who would believe on Him and turn from their evil ways.

The redemption price, they said, was great; but nothing less could have proved so well God's great love for mankind. And they quoted from the Bible, "For God so loved the world, that He gave His only begotten Son, that whosoever believeth in him should not perish, but have everlasting life. For God sent not his Son into the world to condemn the world; but that the world through him might be saved" (John 3:16, 17); also, "The Son of man is come to seek and to save that which was lost" (Luke 19:10). These words were as a soothing balm to John's aching heart. Having been fully awakened to his awful condition and made to long for the way of deliverance, he rejoiced as these rays of hope came streaming down into his soul.

One by one he recalled his sins—smoking and chewing tobacco, drinking whisky and beer, stealing, lying, card-playing, betting, gambling, and many other things; but these he had already given up. One thing only came to his mind that caused him a struggle, and for a few moments it seemed that he could not give that up. John loved to dance, and it had seemed to him that there was nothing wrong with that pastime. Since he knew none of the pleasures that the Christian enjoys, this was not strange. Always he had danced just for the pleasure he derived from dancing, and he considered dancing an innocent amusement. When, however, he was made aware of the evils of dancing and the temptations it causes boys and girls whose characters are weak, he could see how that to some it might mean the loss of virtue; and, too, he found that much of his suffering had been caused by the late hours that dancing and other things had caused him to keep. Then he gladly bade adieu to the dance-hall and all its trivial gaiety.

After he had asked the Lord to pardon him for his transgressions, his simple faith took hold of the promises and he received a clear witness of his acceptance as a child of God. At last, after so many weeks and months—yes, years—of dissatisfaction, he was indeed truly happy; and the deep aching in his hungry heart was replaced by the Savior's love. His companions, too, went away from that service rejoicing. Their language, once so rough and vile, was now becoming to any Christian; and the things that they had loved, no longer attracted their attention. In fact, the entire neighborhood was changed; for many haunts of sin and vice were entirely vacated.

John soon found that it was his duty to make all of his wrongs right as far as it lay in his power to do so; and this he gladly did. In many instances he was surprised to see the effect that this act of obedience had upon the ones concerned. Many, with tears in their eyes, exclaimed, "John, I only wish that I possessed the joy in my own heart that I can see written in your face!"

CHAPTER X
A Child Again

No one could doubt the change in John's life; and many wondered how such a thing could have been accomplished. But they did not realize that with God all things are possible. How well it was for John that he discovered before it was too late that he was a sinner, lost in God's sight, and that it was necessary for him to forsake all of his evil ways and habits if he would be freed from the binding chain of Satan! Each sinful habit formed a link in the chain, and its strength could be measured only by what it took to release him from its binding power.

John was sorry to see the meetings close; and as he bade the sweet-faced women farewell, he was loath to see them go, because of their Christian influence. But life to him was no longer what it had been in the past. With the poet, he had found that

"Life is real! life is earnest.
And the grave is not its goal;
Dust thou art, to dust returnest
Was not spoken of the soul."

He procured a Bible and studied it diligently. He soon found that it was a wonderful book, for what troubled him in one part was explained in another. One day while reading in the tenth chapter of Mark, he found to his surprise that, instead of his being a man, he was only a child, a mere babe, in God's sight. John had expected to be changed and to be different in every way, but he did not know that, in order to realize his desire to be a "man after God's own heart," he must commence at the beginning and be as a little child again. But he was willing; for he saw how his past life had been completely wasted, and he was glad to begin anew.

In the second chapter of I Peter, John found much encouragement, also in I Cor. 13:11, where he read: "When I was a child, I thought as a child: but when I became a man, I put away childish things." Again he was determined to become a man, and to develop as quickly as possible. From that time on he availed himself of every opportunity to do good to all mankind, and this was no hardship. His great whole-hearted nature made him love to do good and to be a help to all who were in need.

At other times John read the conversation between Christ and Nicodemus, and the account of how Jesus thanked his heavenly Father for hiding His truths from the wise and prudent and for revealing them to babes. John was not long in perceiving the mystery concerning the new birth, for he had gained the experience; and he thanked God that it had been revealed to him.

Once while studying the Word of God, John discovered that the twelfth chapter of I Corinthians teaches that Christian people on the earth represent Christ's spiritual body. As the natural body possesses many members—hands, feet, eyes, ears, nose, etc.—each having its own special work, just so the spiritual body of which He (Christ) is the head has many members to carry on the Lord's work on the earth. And, as in the human body, each member has its own work to do; similarly, in the spiritual body, each member has his own work to perform. Some preach, some teach, some perform miracles, some (perhaps all) pray for the sick, and some do various other things, each as he is directed; but all work in harmony. The members are all assigned their work and places in the body by the directions of the heavenly Father.

From reading the second chapter of Acts, John found that soon after Christ ascended to heaven God sent His Holy Spirit to the earth to superintend the work of the members of His Son's spiritual body, or saved people, and that this same Holy Spirit is still guiding and helping them. He also read in I John 2:15—"Love not the world, neither the things that are in the world. If any man love the world, the love of the Father is not in him."

By reading further in the apostle John's epistle, John discovered that there are many false spirits in the world that are trying to deceive God's people and that it is often necessary to try the spirits to know which is right. He saw that the test is love. If anyone loves God and His Son, Jesus, more than anything else in the world, and feels as much interest in his neighbor's welfare as in his own, that one can be sure that he is God's own child. And Paul's letter to the Ephesians tells of an armor that God has prepared for His people to wear that will enable them to overcome all false spirits.

A Sunday-school was soon started in the neighborhood and John was chosen to be the teacher of the infant class. At first he tried to plead his inability, but no one would listen to his excuses. He was glad afterward; for he learned to love the little ones very dearly. While he was meeting with the children Sunday after Sunday, he often thought of many of the hard places through which he had passed when he was a child and remembered that it was because he had not been warned that he had, one step at a time, gone down until he was in misery and on the verge of despair. So John sought to throw light on each one of these dangerous places and to point out the dangers so clearly that the children could plainly see and understand the wrong for themselves before they were beguiled and then bound by Satan's chain of evil habits. In this way he helped the children to escape many a snare by which they might otherwise have been caught unawares.

As the weeks sped by into months and John continued to unfold to the tender questioning minds the hidden mysteries of the Bible, the adult class became interested; and it was not long until they decided that they needed him for their class more than the children did for theirs. While he was teaching the advanced Bible class, his own understanding of spiritual things was greatly broadened and strengthened, and he became one on whom the entire congregation could lean and in whom they could confide.

On one occasion when the lesson was in the epistle of James, John found by reading the fifth chapter of that book that Jesus is just as able and ready to heal those who are sick as He was to relieve sufferers in days gone by and that any who are afflicted may pray expecting to be healed. He quickly applied the Scripture to himself, and began to pray thus:

"Lord, thou seest how I am afflicted because of the sinful habits that I formed in my childhood. Thou hast now taken from me the desire for these things, but the suffering in my back and lungs is so intense. Lord Jesus, heal me! Make me well, and I will work for Thee all the days of my life!"

God answered that prayer and made him strong and well; then he could say with the Psalmist, "Bless the Lord, O my soul, and forget not all his benefits: who forgiveth all thine iniquities; who healeth all thy diseases." Oh, the goodness of the Lord to John! He felt that he never could cease praising Him.

The sad and lonely past, the days of his vain struggles to become the man that his earthly father had desired him to be, could never be compared to these days of happiness, the days when his desires to attain to true manhood were being realized. His heart was lonely no longer. He had a Friend who was dearer than a mother could have been. And he felt that it is a wonderful privilege to be a member in Christ's body, the church.

CHAPTER XI
How John Became a Man

As the news of John's wonderful conversion and of his work among the people spread throughout the country, it reached the ears of Farmer Z, in whose home John for the first time had attended family worship. The kind-hearted man had never forgotten the boy who had endeavored to make his escape to the barn rather than to come into the sitting-room at the worship hour, and he felt a desire to have a good heart-to-heart visit with John and to know just how he came to find the Lord. John was, therefore, very much surprised one day to hear that this good gentleman, of whom he had in the past been so fearful, was desiring to see him. But he was glad; for he, too, had felt a great desire to talk with Farmer Z, the one who was first to open his heart to a ray of heavenly sunshine.

"I have been hearing wonderful stories about you of late, my boy," the farmer said as John approached him; and as he took the young man's hand, his hearty handshake sent the blood tingling through John's veins. "Come," the farmer continued, "sit down and tell me what it was that brought about the change. My boy, I understand that you are already getting to be quite a preacher. Is it true?"

"Well, Mr. Z," John modestly replied, "I hardly know what answer to make, except that it was the work of my Savior. I am like the poor beggar who was blind—'one thing I know, that, whereas I was blind, now I see.' The same Jesus that healed the blind man has opened my spiritual eyes, making me to see and understand what never before seemed possible."

Then as John related some of his Christian experiences, the farmer was made to wonder at the loving-kindness and the great mercy of his God.

"John," he said, as he looked into the beaming eyes of the young man and noted the boyish face but manly form (for there was scarcely a trace of the early dissipation left), "I see that you have found the genuine article. God has worked a miracle in your life, and I guess he wants you to go and tell the world about it. How is it, my boy? Do you feel like preaching the gospel?"

And then it was that John, in his simple, earnest manner, for which he was so loved and admired, said:

"Mr. Z, I feel as though some power within me is leading me about; and I long to tell everyone I meet of the Jesus, who so loved the lost world that He laid down His life upon the cross. It seems I can think of little else."

"That's it! That's it!" Farmer Z exclaimed; "God has put His Holy Spirit in your heart and has called you into His harvest-field to go forth and help spread the gospel. Go, my boy; and may God speed your footsteps in ways crowned with blessings of success. I rejoice with you in your calling and shall pray for you. When trials come your way—and they will— remember that there is always a light in God's window for the faithful, a light that will guide them safely home at last. Remember also that He has said, 'Be thou faithful unto death.'"

When the farmer bade John adieu, the sun had disappeared beyond the horizon and the crimson shades were gathering in the western sky. The landscape that stretched before him was beautiful. And while John was not unconscious of these beautiful surroundings, by his inner vision, which could not be limited by the vast prairie country with its varied possibilities, he looked upon another scene far beyond—he saw the heavenly city, the New Jerusalem, once beheld by the sainted John; and he wondered what could be more grand and majestic.

John had at last developed into a noble-hearted Christian, whose greatest desire in life was to please his God, and to spend his time wholly in God's service; and one day a few years later he stood on the deck of a large Atlantic steamer and waved farewell to his friends on the shore. He was bound for a far-distant land; God was sending him as a missionary to carry the gospel to the people of another country.

His large brown eyes, sorrowful no longer, were dimmed by tears of farewell; but the tears only made them shine the brighter. They witnessed to the gladness of his heart; and to the eagerness within his bosom pushing him forward.

John had at last become a man after God's own heart.